This Walker book belongs to

....

For Billy and Michelle
and Denise, Louise and Nic

First published 2011 by Walker Books Ltd

87 Vauxhall Walk, London SE11 5HJ

This edition published 2012

2 4 6 8 10 9 7 5 3 1

© 2011 Fiona Ross

The right of Fiona Ross to be identified as author/illustrator of this work has been
asserted by her in accordance with the Copyright, Designs and Patents Act 1988

This book has been typeset in WB Fiona Ross

Printed in China

British Library Cataloguing in Publication Data:
a catalogue record for this book is available from the British Library

ISBN 978-1-4063-3855-3

www.walker.co.uk

Chilly Milly Moo

Fiona Ross

WALKER BOOKS
AND SUBSIDIARIES

LONDON · BOSTON · SYDNEY · AUCKLAND

Milly Moo the cow was sad.
"What's up?" mooed the other cows.

Milly Moo the cow was glum.

"What's up?" asked the farmer.

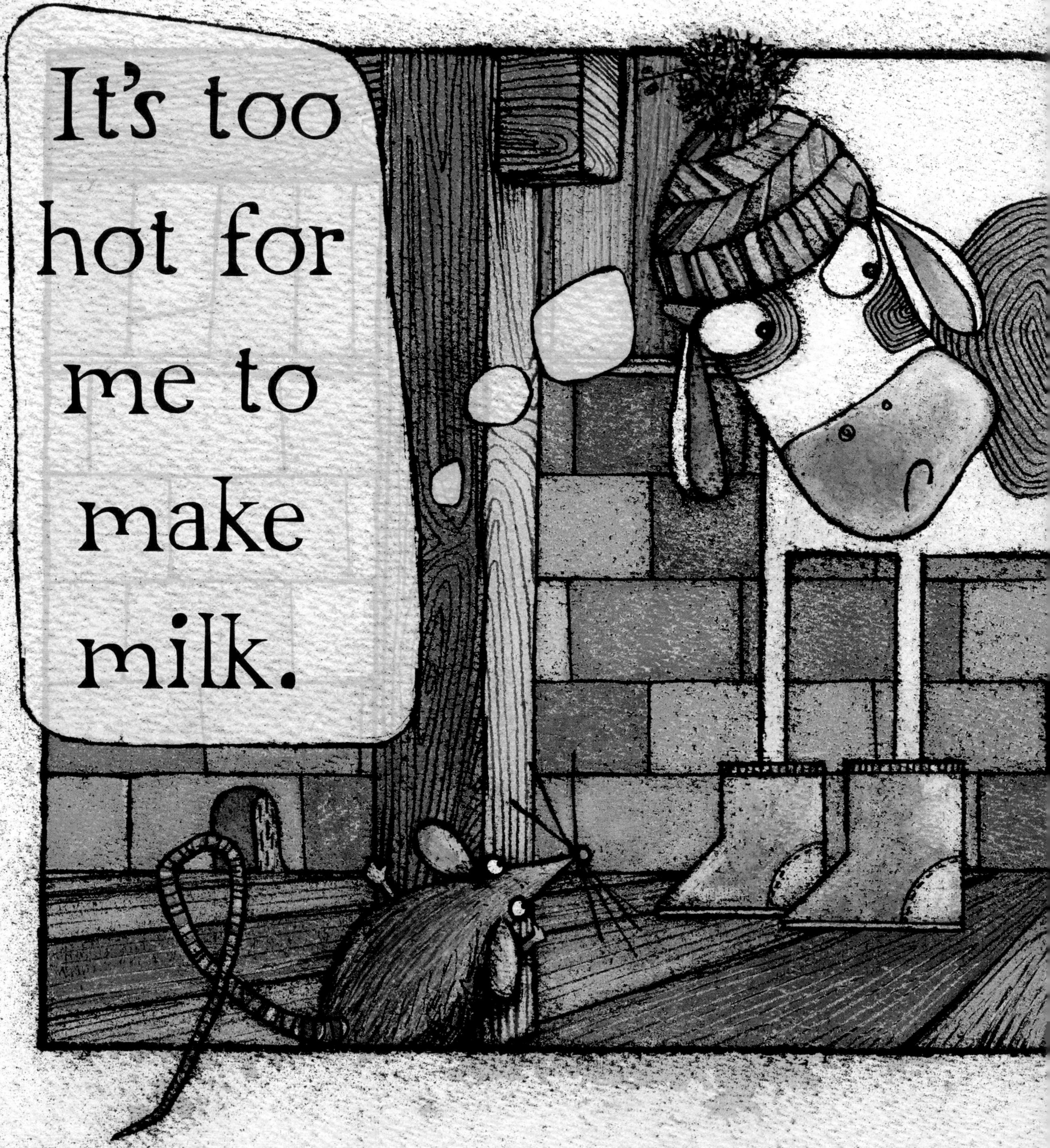
It's too hot for me to make milk.

Milly Moo wanted to churn out the finest, loveliest, tastiest, creamiest milk.

But she couldn't.

"You can't stay here if you can't make milk," said the farmer.

"Aw, what a poor cow! The sun helps us make milk," boasted the others.

The other cows sniggered. They couldn't understand why Milly Moo was different.

That night Milly Moo dreamed about what might happen to her.

Where did cows go that couldn't make milk?

She
woke
to find a storm
was
raging.

It was getting colder.

"Let's have one last try!"

Strange noises erupted from Milly Moo.

BUBBLE

BABBLE

There was an explosion of the coldest, chilliest, frostiest, iciest ...

The other cows
wished that they could
be like Milly Moo.

We can't make ice cream!

"Don't be misery moos," said Milly Moo.

"We're all special!"
said Milly Moo.
"It's just that I like being chilly.
Let's go and enjoy the big freeze!"

The End